ISADORA MOON

Has a Birthday

Harriet Muncaster

A STEPPING STONE BOOK™

Random House 🏠 New York

For vampires, fairies, and humans everywhere!
And for Georgina, my favorite sister.

Copyright © 2016 by Harriet Muncaster
Cover art copyright © 2016 by Harriet Muncaster

All rights reserved. Published in the United States by Random House
Children's Books, a division of Penguin Random House LLC, New York.
Originally published in paperback by Oxford University Press,
Oxford, in 2016.

Random House and the colophon are registered trademarks and
A Stepping Stone Book and the colophon are trademarks of
Penguin Random House LLC.

Visit us on the Web!
SteppingStonesBooks.com
rhcbooks.com

Educators and librarians, for a variety of teaching tools,
visit us at RHTeachersLibrarians.com

Library of Congress Cataloging-in-Publication Data is available upon request.
ISBN 978-0-399-55833-7 (hc)—ISBN 978-0-399-55835-1 (pbk.)—
ISBN 978-0-399-55836-8 (ebook)

MANUFACTURED IN CHINA
10 9 8 7 6 5 4 3 2 1
First American Edition

This book has been officially leveled by using the
F&P Text Level Gradient™ Leveling System.

ISADORA MOON

Has a Birthday

Chapter One

Isadora Moon, that's me! And this is Pink Rabbit. He was my favorite stuffed animal, so Mom brought him to life with her wand. He comes everywhere with me, even to birthday parties!

I have been to lots of birthday parties since I started school. Human ones! They are very interesting and very different from the parties we have at home. I had only ever been to vampire or fairy ones before I met my human friends. That's because my mom is a fairy and my dad is a vampire. Yes, really!

Do you know what that makes me?

A vampire-fairy!

Being half-fairy, half-vampire isn't easy—I wasn't sure where I fit in! But then I went to human school and discovered that *everyone* is a little different and that's the best way to be.

I have really enjoyed going to my human friends' birthday parties. They are all so different! I couldn't wait for my birthday so that I could have a party of my own.

"I hope you will be having a nice traditional vampire party when it's your birthday," said Dad.

"Hmm," I said.

I wasn't sure about having a vampire

party. I think my friends would find it a little scary. A vampire party is always held in the dead of night, and you have to dress very fancy and have neat hair. Vampires are very fussy about their appearance. They like to play flying games and shoot across the sky at lightning-quick speed. My wings can never keep up, because they are more flappy, like fairy wings. Vampires also like to eat red food at their parties and drink red juice. I don't like red food.

"How about a nice traditional fairy party?" suggested Mom. "That would be fun!"

I remembered the fairy party I had when I was four. It was a swimming party. Fairies love nature, so we went to a wild forest stream. It was very cold, and there were lots of weeds and fish in the water.

"It's so refreshing!" Mom cried as she jumped into the water with all the fairy guests.

I shivered in the water. Pink Rabbit stood on a rock. He hates getting wet.

"I'd rather have a human party like my

friends at school," I told Mom and Dad honestly. "They are much more fun."

"Impossible," said Dad. "There's nothing more fun than a vampire party. Think of all the delicious red food!"

"I think another swimming party would be wonderful," said Mom dreamily. "We could have a campfire afterward and make flower crowns."

"I would really like a human party," I said. "Please? At a human party there are all kinds of fun things!"

"What kinds of fun things?" asked Mom suspiciously.

"Well, at Zoe's party last week we all had to wear costumes."

"I wondered why you were wearing those pink bunny ears," said Dad.

"I was being Pink Rabbit!" I told him. "And Pink Rabbit dressed up as me. It was so much fun. We had cake and ice cream, and there were party favors, and we played hot potato."

"What potato?" asked Mom.

"Hot potato!" I said. "You pass a present around and around in a circle, and at the end there's a surprise!"

"Sounds very weird," said Mom. "And what is a party favor?"

"It's a bag you give the guests at the end of the party," I explained. "It's full of little presents."

I continued, "At Oliver's birthday party, he had a bouncy castle and a magician."

"A magician sounds good," said Mom, perking up.

"A pretend one," I said quickly. "He didn't do real magic like you can do with your wand."

Mom looked confused. "Why not?" she asked.

I shrugged. "It's just the way they do it at human parties."

"It all sounds very strange," said Dad.

"I really would love a human birthday party," I said, smiling my most angelic smile.

Mom and Dad sighed.

"Well . . . all right, then," said Mom.

"I guess we could try a human birthday party this year," agreed Dad.

Pink Rabbit and I jumped up and down in excitement.

"Thank you! Thank you!" I shouted. Pink Rabbit can't shout, but he waved his paws in the air.

Chapter Two

When it came to planning my birthday party, Mom and Dad seemed to be organized.

"We don't need any help," they said.

"Are you sure you know what you're doing?" I asked nervously.

"Oh yes!" said Dad. "We've got all the ideas written down: hot potato, magician, cake, balloons, presents, bouncy castle, costumes, party favors. . . ."

"It's going to be the best birthday party ever!" said Mom.

"Don't forget the invitations," I told them.

Dad frowned and scratched his head. Then he wrote "invitations" at the bottom of the list.

The next day at school we were doing math problems when suddenly we could hear a flapping sound from outside.

"What on earth is that?" said Miss Cherry, darting toward the window.

A swarm of envelopes flew through the air on bat wings. They were tapping against the windows, trying to get in.

"Oh my!" Miss Cherry exclaimed.

I felt my face go red with embarrassment.

"Let them in!" cried Oliver. "Let's see what they are!"

"Don't let them in!" wailed Samantha.

The envelopes kept beating their wings against the glass until one of them found an open window. It beckoned to the others. Then they all came flying in, fluttering and flapping, landing one by one on my friends' desks.

"It's an invitation!" cried Oliver once he had ripped his envelope open.

"A birthday party!" yelled Zoe. "At Isadora's house!"

"It's a costume party!" someone else said.

All the kids were talking excitedly, but

18

Miss Cherry did not look happy. In fact, she seemed annoyed.

"Isadora," she said. "It's not appropriate to make such a scene in the middle of a lesson."

I slunk down in my chair and felt like I wanted to disappear.

"Sorry," I whispered.

DEAR: Oliver

You're invited to
Isadora Moon's Birthday Party!

WHEN: This Saturday

WHERE: The big pink-and-black house

TIME: 10 AM – 3 PM

RSVP

PS Please wear a costume!

* ★ *

When I got home that afternoon, I marched into the kitchen, where Mom and Dad were busy making party decorations.

"You got me into trouble at school, sending those bat invitations," I told them.

Dad looked surprised.

"But they were so good," he said. "Did you see how I used my very best handwriting?"

"Did your friends like them?" asked Mom.

"Well, yes . . . ," I said. "But they weren't like normal human party invitations, you know."

"They weren't?" asked Mom.

"No!" I said. "With human invitations you just hand them out yourself. They're

20

only made of paper—they don't have wings."

"How boring," said Dad, who was in the middle of sticking stars onto a "Happy Birthday" banner.

Happy Birthday

"You are planning a *human* birthday party, aren't you?" I asked nervously.

"Yes," said Dad. "Don't worry, Isadora. We have it all under control." He tapped his list of ideas. "We are following your instructions exactly."

I peeked at the list again. "Hot potato, magician, cake, balloons, presents, bouncy castle, costumes, party favors."

"Invitations" was crossed out.

"Okay," I said, feeling reassured once again. "But you know you don't have to include all those things in the party. Most human parties just have one or two."

"Of course," said Dad absentmindedly.

I made myself a peanut butter sandwich and headed upstairs to my bedroom in the tower.

Chapter Three

On the morning of my birthday, I woke up bright and early. The sun was shining outside, and the birds were chirping. I poked Pink Rabbit awake.

"Today's the day!" I said to him. I leapt out of bed, and we flew down the stairs together.

Mom, Dad, and my baby sister, Honeyblossom, were all in the kitchen waiting for me. The table had been set for breakfast, and sitting in front of my place was a pink package tied up with glittery ribbon.

"Happy birthday, Isadora!" cried Mom and Dad together. They both sat at the table, smiling. Mom had a bowl of flower-nectar yogurt with wild berries in front of her, and Dad had already started drinking his red juice. Vampires love red juice. Honeyblossom was sitting in her high chair and happily waving her bottle of pink milk in the air.

I sat down at the table.

"May I open my present?" I asked excitedly.

"Of course!" said Mom. "You have only one because it's a very, very special gift this year."

I reached for the present. I was just about to pick it up and tear off the wrapping when . . .

DING DONG!

Mom swooped the present away from under my hands and jumped to her feet.

"That must be Cousin Wilbur!" she said. "He's here early. We can't let him see Isadora's present. He'll be very jealous."

She put my present in the cupboard under the sink and hurried to answer the door.

"You'll have to open it later," said Dad, sounding disappointed.

Cousin Wilbur came into the room. He was wearing a long black robe with silver stars on it and a pointy hat on his head. Wilbur is a wizard. Well, almost a wizard. He is a wizard-in-training and also a bossy know-it-all. He thinks he knows everything because he is older than me.

"Happy birthday, Isadora," he said. Then he puffed out his chest and stuck his nose in the air in a smug sort of way.

"I am your birthday magician," he explained. "Wilbur the Great!"

"But . . . ," I began.

"I have some excellent tricks up my sleeve," Wilbur continued. "Your friends will all be very impressed."

"It's very nice of you to come and help out at Isadora's party," said Mom.

"It is, isn't it," agreed Wilbur.

I frowned. "Wilbur is a real magician," I said. "The magician is only supposed to do pretend magic."

Mom, Dad, and Wilbur all looked confused.

"Well, that's just silly," snorted Wilbur. "Can a human magician do this?"

He took his hat off and held it in front of him. Then he said a very long and complicated word and stuck his hand into the hat. . . .

"ARGHHHH!" he yelled. "Get it OFF!"

From the end of Wilbur's finger, holding on by its teeth, dangled a large white rabbit. Wilbur swung his arm around and around.

"GET IT OFF!" he screamed.

Pink Rabbit put his paws over his eyes, and Honeyblossom started to cry. Mom picked up her wand from the breakfast table and waved it. The white rabbit vanished into thin air.

Wilbur continued to swing his arm around and scream for a while longer

before realizing the rabbit had disappeared.
Wilbur's face went bright red—as red as his
sore finger.

"Ahem," he said. "I might have to practice that trick."

"Yes, that might be a good idea," said Dad hurriedly. "Why don't you go and do a little bit of practice before the guests arrive?"

"It won't be long now," said Mom, looking at the clock. "There's a lot to fit in today, so we asked everyone to arrive early. Isadora, you had better go and change into your costume!"

Chapter Four

I felt butterflies of excitement flutter in my stomach. It was almost time for my party! I grabbed Pink Rabbit's paw, and we ran upstairs to change. As I put my costume on, I started to feel nervous. Would my friends think my family was too weird? And what would they think of Cousin Wilbur?

"Bewitching!" said Dad when I came downstairs in my costume. "You look just like a bat!"

I loved my outfit. Dad had helped me to make it the night before. I had some black velvet ears on a headband, and a black spiky dress, and even some black bat shoes in the shape of claws. I twirled with Pink Rabbit in the hallway until . . .

DING DONG!

The first guest had arrived! It was Zoe. She was wearing a black catsuit and standing on the doorstep with her mom.

"Happy birthday, Isadora!" she said. She handed me a present wrapped up with a big pink bow.

"Thank you, Zoe!" I said happily.

Zoe's mom peered curiously into the hallway.

"I see your parents dressed up too, Isadora," she said. "How fun! That's a nice fairy costume your mom is wearing. The wings look so realistic! And what a great job they've done decorating the house! The bat chandelier is a nice touch for the party."

"It's not just for the party . . . ," I started to explain, but Zoe's mom was looking at her watch.

"I have to go," she said. "I'll be back to

pick you up later, Zoe!" She gave Zoe a quick
kiss on the cheek and hurried down the
garden path.

Oliver was next to arrive. He was dressed as a vampire.

"Wonderful!" said Dad when he saw Oliver's costume. "I didn't know you had invited any vampires, Isadora!"

"He's not a real . . . ," I began.

"I had better get some red juice for the vampire," said Dad, hurrying toward the fridge.

The doorbell chimed again, and Mom opened the door. Shy Samantha stood on the doorstep, dressed as a fairy.

"Oooh!" squeaked Mom. "I didn't realize you had invited any fairies, Isadora! How wonderful. We can talk all about nature!" She took Samantha's hand and led her into the kitchen.

★ ★ ★

When all my friends had arrived, we went into the great hall. Mom and Dad had done a fantastic job decorating it.

Silver stars hung from the ceiling, and there were pink and black balloons all over the floor.

My friends seemed very impressed. Some

of them were running around the room and playing with the balloons. They all looked happy.

Maybe my party will be fun, just like a human one after all! I thought.

Chapter
Five

"Time for hot potato!" boomed Dad, who had put on a pair of fancy sunglasses to protect his eyes from the morning light. It was still very early for him to be awake. Vampires usually sleep through the day.

"You all know the rules, don't you?" he shouted. "Of course you do. You're humans!"

Then he produced a big present from behind his back.

"Everyone in a circle, please!" he said.

My friends and I shuffled ourselves into a circle on the floor, and Dad gave the package to one of my friends.

"There you are," he said. "Pass it around."

We all started to pass the present around the circle. But something was missing.

"Music!" I whispered to Dad. "We need music!"

"Music!" shouted Dad to Mom.

Mom opened her mouth and started to sing a tinkly fairy song. I felt my face go red with embarrassment. Some of my friends started to giggle.

"That's right! It's a hot potato!" called Dad.
"Pass it around. Around and around it goes!"

The "hot potato" present went around and
around the circle. And then it went around

and around again! I started to wonder when Mom was going to stop singing. I was about to whisper to Dad again when suddenly there was a great big **BANG**.

"SURPRISE!" shouted Dad as the package exploded in Oliver's hands. Fireworks shot out of it and up into the air.

Glittery pink sparks and sparkling, fizzing stars swirled and whirled around the room.

"Oh no!" I said to Pink Rabbit.

But my friends didn't seem to mind. In fact, they liked it. They all stood up and started dancing to Mom's song under the falling sparks.

"They're so pretty!" breathed Zoe as she tried to catch a shooting star.

"It's magical!" yelled Sashi.

Everyone danced until the sparks stopped falling and Mom stopped singing.

"Time for the magician," announced Dad, opening the door for Wilbur. He swept in, swishing his starry robe.

"It's Wilbur the Great, actually," corrected Wilbur. "Sit down, everyone," he said bossily. "Today I am going to show you a wonderful trick. Who wants to be turned into a box of frogs?"

I groaned. A boy from my class named Bruno put his hand in the air, and Wilbur gestured for Bruno to come and stand next to him.

Wilbur rolled up his sleeves, closed his eyes, and puffed out his chest importantly. Then he pointed his finger at Bruno.

"ALLIKAZAMBANANA!" he said.

There was a loud **BANG** and a puff of pink smoke.

Bruno disappeared, and in his place stood a large cardboard box. Loud croaking sounds were coming from inside.

"WOW!" said my friends. "AMAZING!"

"It's like real magic!" said Oliver.

We all watched as frogs started to jump out of the box. Wilbur looked very pleased with himself.

"Look at them all!" squealed Zoe as the frogs started to hop away across the room.

47

"Eww," said Samantha. "I hate frogs."

"What next?" asked Wilbur. "Who wants to see me pull a rabbit from my hat?"

Everyone cheered except Pink Rabbit, who looked very worried.

Wilbur put on some thick gloves. "Just in case it bites," he said, winking, and everyone laughed.

"Wilbur," I called out worriedly. "What about Bruno?"

"What about him?" said Wilbur, starting to put his gloved hand into his hat.

"Shouldn't you turn him back now?" I asked.

Wilbur looked surprised.

48

"Oh," he said. "Well, yes. I guess I should."

He took his hand out of his hat. He was holding a fluffy white rat.

"That's not a rabbit!" shouted Oliver,

laughing. "That's a rat!" All my friends were laughing now. They thought Wilbur was hilarious.

"Oh," said Wilbur, disappointed. "So it is."

"WILBUR!" I shouted. "You need to turn Bruno back into a boy!"

"All right," said Wilbur, looking annoyed. "You'll have to catch the frogs, though. If you forget one, then Bruno might come back missing an ear or something."

My friends and I went off in search of the frogs.

"We can't send Bruno home with only one ear!" I wailed.

50

"Let me help!" said Mom, holding her wand up in the air. But Wilbur did not want any help.

"No, no," he said. "I can do it!"

At last all the frogs were collected and back in the box. We stared expectantly at Wilbur. He seemed a little nervous.

"Don't stare at me," he ordered. "It breaks my concentration."

Wilbur turned around so that he had his back to everyone and waved his arms in the air. We all waited. There were a few loud bangs and a lot of smoke, but eventually Bruno appeared.

"Ribbit," he said.

"Oops! Hang on," said Wilbur. He waved

his hands again and said some more magic
words.

Bruno blinked and looked confused, but
this time when he opened his mouth, words
came out instead of croaks.

"That was awesome!" he said.

I breathed a sigh of relief.

"Thank goodness for that!" said Dad, swooping in. "I think it's time for the next activity."

"But I haven't finished my show, Uncle Bartholomew," said Wilbur crossly.

"I think you have," said Dad firmly. "I think we will move on to the bouncy castle now."

I smiled. A bouncy castle! Nothing could go wrong with that. There was still time for my party to be like a real human one.

Chapter Six

We all followed Mom and Dad into the back garden. Then Mom pointed her wand at the sky. A silvery thread shot out of the end and lassoed itself around one of the fat, fluffy clouds in the sky. Mom pulled the cloud down to the ground gently and stuck it into the grass.

"Clouds make wonderful alternatives to bouncy castles," she told everyone. "So much softer and bouncier."

I frowned. I should have known a human bouncy castle was too much to ask for.

But my friends didn't seem to mind. They all looked astonished and excited. Their eyes were round like saucers.

"You can all hop on," said Mom. "Bounce away! We are going to go inside to put the candles on the birthday cake."

Zoe was the first to take off her shoes and jump onto the cloud.

"It's so soft!" she exclaimed as she bounced
up and down. "I'm so high!"

Soon all my friends were on the cloud,
bouncing around and laughing. It didn't look
like anything could go wrong this time, so
I decided to join in. I climbed onto the cloud
and started jumping.

57

"Whee!" I cried.

Suddenly, I felt very happy. Everyone was having a good time. Even Samantha! It was just as much fun as a regular human party!

"It's like flying!" yelled Oliver.

As we soared higher and laughed and screamed, I noticed Wilbur come out of the house and into the garden. He walked over to the cloud and stared up at us.

"Do you want me to make it even bouncier?" he asked. "Seeing as I didn't get to finish my show, I could do some more magic for you now."

"Oh yes!" cried my friends. "Please do more magic!"

I stopped bouncing and jumped right off the cloud and onto the grass.

"I don't think that's a good idea, Wilbur," I began.

"Why not?" said Wilbur. "It will be much more fun if it's bouncier. Here, let me do some more magic."

He rolled up his starry sleeves and waved his arms in the air.

"**KABOOOOOOMMMSKA!**" he said, and a shower of sparks shot out of his fingers.

The cloud gave a little wobble, and my friends began to fly up higher and higher into the air.

"Wow!" Bruno cried. "This is amazing! It IS bouncier! Look at me!"

"See?" said Wilbur. "Much more fun!" He crossed his arms and looked down at me. "You should just relax, Isadora," he said.

But I couldn't relax. Something didn't seem right. The cloud was rocking and shaking. It couldn't handle the added amount of bounce. The cloud began to loosen from its pegs.

"Everyone, get off!" I shouted in a panic. But no one listened to me. They were all having too much fun. I tugged on Wilbur's sleeve.

"Look!" I said. "It's about to fly away!"

"It's not going to fly away!" said Wilbur, rolling his eyes.

"It is!" I insisted, pointing at the pegs stuck into the grass. One by one the strings that were tied to the pegs snapped, and slowly the cloud began to rise up into the air—with all of my friends on it!

"Oh," said Wilbur, staring in horror. "Whoops."

"I told you!" I said crossly.

We watched as the cloud floated higher
and higher.

"Do something!" I said to Wilbur.

"I can't bring a cloud down from the sky!"
he said. "I won't learn how to do that until
next term at wizard school."

"I'll get Mom. You stay here and don't move!" I shouted.

I ran to the kitchen, where Dad was putting the last few candles into an enormous cake.

"Whoa, Isadora, you're not supposed to see the cake yet!" he said.

"It's an emergency!" I told him. "Where's Mom?"

"She had to run upstairs for a minute,"

said Dad. "Honeyblossom was crying and needed some pink milk."

"Oh no, oh no!" I wailed.

"What's wrong?" asked Dad.

I was going to explain, when I saw the very thing I needed sitting on the kitchen table: Mom's wand. I grabbed it and flew back outside.

Chapter Seven

Wilbur was still standing where I had left him, staring at the sky.

"There it is," he said to me, pointing at a speck in the distance. It looked so small and so far away. There was no time to lose. I flapped my wings and rose up into the air.

I flew as fast as I could—faster than

ever before—but it still took a long time to catch up with the cloud. At last I was near enough to hear my friends' voices. They had all stopped bouncing now. They were sitting very still and looked very scared. Some of them were lying on their stomachs with their faces peering over the edge. Their eyes were big and round as they stared down at the ground miles and miles below. Pink Rabbit had his paws over his eyes.

"Isadora!" called Zoe as I landed gently on the cloud and sat down to get my breath back. "We thought you were never coming!"

"We thought we were lost in the sky forever!" said Oliver.

Pink Rabbit just bounced over to me and put his paws around my legs.

"I'm sorry," I said. "It was my cousin Wilbur. He should never have put more magic on the cloud."

"But we're safe now that you're here, aren't we?" asked Samantha.

I wasn't so sure—I am only half-fairy, and wand magic isn't my strong point—but

69

I made myself smile as though it was completely normal to be stuck on top of a cloud in the middle of the sky.

"Oh yes," I said. "Don't worry. I'll find a way to get us down. I've got my mom's wand." I held it up in the air, and the pink star glittered in the sunlight.

"Great!" said Oliver. "We're saved!"

I felt nervous as I closed my eyes. I wasn't sure if I could get the cloud and all my friends back down to the ground, but I had to try.

In my mind, I pictured the cloud floating gently back down to earth. Then I waved the wand and opened my eyes.

Nothing had happened.

Oh no, I thought anxiously. I closed my eyes to try again. I concentrated on the cloud harder this time. I imagined it sinking down, down, down. . . . I waved the wand as hard as I could.

But when I opened my eyes again, nothing had happened.

"Oh no," I said aloud.

"What is it?" asked Samantha in a small, scared voice.

"I don't know if I can do it," I said truthfully. "This is big magic. I can only really do small kinds of wand magic. And . . . and I don't always get my spells right."

I remembered the time at fairy school when I had tried to make a carrot cake appear. All I had managed was a carrot with bat wings that flew around the room and caused chaos.

"How will we get down?" said Samantha, sounding frightened.

"We have to think of another way," said Zoe. "There must be another way."

Samantha screwed up her eyes as though she was thinking very hard. Then she opened them again and looked a little less panicked.

"You know what my mom always tells me," she said. "She says that sometimes it's the little things that make a difference. So maybe it will only take a little bit of magic to get us out of this big mess. We have to think of a spell you CAN do!"

She pointed at the wings of her fairy costume. "Could you make these come alive?" she asked.

I looked at the wings. They were very small compared to the cloud.

"I can try," I said.

Samantha looked around at all our friends sitting on the cloud in their costumes. She pointed at Bruno in his dragon suit.

"Do you think you could use magic to make Bruno's dragon wings really work too?" she asked.

I looked at the two fabric wings sewn on the back of Bruno's costume.

"Maybe!" I said, feeling excited. "Yes, I think I could do that!"

"Well then, I have an idea," said Samantha. "Look how many of us have wings on our costumes. Bruno has dragon wings, I have fairy wings, Sashi has butterfly wings, Oliver has a cape, and, of course, you have real wings! If you could bring all the wings to life, then half of us would be able to fly."

"We could all help each other to fly back to my yard!" I said. "Samantha, you're a genius!" I gave her a big hug, and her face went as pink as Mom's hair.

"Let's try it," I said.

75

Chapter Eight

We started with Bruno. I pointed Mom's wand at his dragon wings and imagined them flapping to life. At first it didn't work.

The wings just changed color and then were covered in polka dots, but after a few tries they gave a little twitch and flapped to life. Bruno immediately rose up into the air.

"Wow!" he yelled. "Look at me!"

I tried Samantha's fairy wings next. It took only two tries before they started to flap.

"Eeek!" squealed Samantha as she rose into the air.

"It's working!" shouted Zoe excitedly, though I could tell she

was a little jealous that she had not chosen a costume with wings.

I had got the hang of the wand now, and the last two spells were easy. Oliver and Sashi rose up into the air, shrieking with delight.

"Okay, everyone," I said. "We all have to help each other now. The ones who can fly should hold hands with the ones who can't."

I took Zoe's hand with one of mine and held on to Pink Rabbit's paw with the other. Soon all of us were floating.

"We must stick together," I said to everyone.

"I'm scared!" said Samantha, looking fearfully down at the ground. It seemed very far away. The houses and trees looked tiny, like little models.

"Don't be frightened, Samantha," I reassured her. "Flying is fun!"

"It is fun!" agreed Bruno. "I wish I could fly all the time!"

"I LOVE flying!" cried Oliver.

Together, we all flapped slowly away from the cloud. There was nothing beneath

us now. Just air. Of course I am used to that, but my friends were not.

"EEEK!" squeaked Samantha.

"Whoa!" said Oliver.

I pointed at a pink-and-black speck in the distance.

"Look," I said. "That's my house! That's where we need to go. Follow me!"

I flew to the head of the group with Zoe

and Pink Rabbit. Flap, flap, flap went my
little bat wings.

"I can see our school," said Zoe. "And
there's the park! It all looks different from
up here."

"Everything is so small!" said Sashi.

We were getting closer to my house now.
I could just make out my bedroom window.
In the yard there were three dots moving

back and forth. Mom, Dad, and Wilbur. They were waving their arms. Suddenly, two of them shot up into the air and flew toward us.

"Oh my goodness," said Mom when she reached us. "We were so worried!"

"SO worried," added Dad. "We didn't know where the cloud had gone. By the time we came out into the yard, it had disappeared!"

"Disappeared completely!" said Mom. "Oh, I'm so glad you're safe."

We all flew over the garden fence and landed gently back on the grass.

"Wilbur explained what happened," said Dad, giving Wilbur a stern look. "It was very brave of you to go and rescue your friends, Isadora."

"It wasn't just me," I said. "It was Samantha. If it hadn't been for her brilliant idea, we would still be stuck on the cloud. Samantha really saved the day."

"Well then," said Mom. "Thank you, Samantha! Let's all give her three cheers!"

Everyone cheered for Samantha, and her face turned bright pink again. But I could tell she was proud and pleased.

"It maybe wasn't the best idea to use a cloud instead of a bouncy castle," said Mom. "I just got carried away. I'm sorry. I should have ordered a regular bouncy castle. Next time I will."

"NO!" shouted all my friends.

"The cloud was more fun," added Sashi.

"We will try to be more normal from now on," said Dad. "We can see this party

has been quite stressful for you, Isadora."

"NO!" shouted all my friends again.

"Please don't change," pleaded Zoe. "We love you and your family the way you are, Isadora."

"Yes, we do!" said Oliver. "We love that your family is different."

"Just keep being you!" said Bruno.

I looked around at everyone and felt a big smile spread over my face. I couldn't help it. I was just so happy! I even smiled at Cousin Wilbur.

"Really?" I said. "You don't even mind that we got stuck on a cloud in the middle of the sky?"

"It was much more fun than a regular bouncy castle!" said Oliver.

"But I *am* hungry now," said Bruno.

"Then it must be time for cake!" said Dad.

Chapter Nine

Everyone followed Dad back into the house and into the kitchen. A giant cake stood in the middle of the table, decorated all over with stars and bats and stripes. Hundreds of candles were stuck into the icing.

"That's a lot of candles!" said Samantha.

"It's the way they do it at vampire and fairy parties," I explained proudly.

Mom and Dad smiled down at me, and then everyone started to sing.

"Happy birthday to you, happy birthday to you, happy biiiirthday, Isadoraaa . . ."

I tried hard to blow out all the candles. It took a long time, and in the end everyone had to join in.

Dad started to cut the cake.

"This top layer is the red layer," he said. "Specially for vampires." He handed a piece to Oliver.

"The second layer is for fairies," said Mom. "It's got flower petals in it and changes flavor whenever you take a bite." She cut a

slice from the fairy layer and handed it to Samantha.

"The rest is regular human cake," said Dad. "Who wants a slice?"

Everyone put up their hands, but no one wanted to eat the regular human cake. They all wanted a slice of the fairy and vampire layers.

"It's so yummy!" said Oliver.

"You'd better have some red juice to wash it down with," said Dad, handing him a carton from the fridge.

"This has been the most exciting party ever!" said Zoe happily.

90

"I'm sad it's almost over," said Samantha.

"Well, you can't leave without your party favors," said Dad, hurrying out to get them. He came back and handed one to each of my friends.

"Ooh," said Sashi, pulling something out of her bag. "What's this?"

"It's a packet of seeds," said Mom. "To grow your own flowers. Nature is very important."

"I've got a pot of hair gel!" yelled Bruno.

"I've got a flower crown," said Samantha.

"I've got some toothpaste in mine," said Oliver, puzzled.

"That's special toothpaste," said Dad. "It keeps your vampire fangs nice and white. Very important!"

Oliver looked surprised. "But my vampire fangs are just pretend ones!" he said. He put his hand to his mouth and pulled out a set of

plastic fangs. Dad's eyes nearly popped out of his head.

"Wh-wha . . . !?" he stuttered.

"I bought them from the costume shop," said Oliver. "They only cost fifty cents."

"Fifty cents!" Dad gasped. "The nerve!"

He was still recovering from his shock when the doorbell started to ring. It was time for my friends to go home.

Chapter Ten

Zoe was the last to leave.

"Goodbye, Isadora," she said, giving me a warm hug. "Thank you for having me!"

"Thank you for coming!" I said. And I meant it.

Zoe disappeared down the front path with her mom.

"Phew!" said Dad, leaning against the door. "I'm exhausted!"

"Me too," said Mom.

Wilbur slunk into the hallway.

"I'm leaving now too, Uncle and Auntie," he said.

"Ah, Wilbur!" said Dad. "I forgot you were still here. Thank you for your . . . help today."

Wilbur looked a bit sheepish as he fiddled with his starry wizard hat.

"Ahem," he said. "You're welcome."

Then he looked at me.

"Sorry, Isadora," he said gruffly. "I should have listened to you more today."

Then he scooted quickly out the front door before I could say anything. I was shocked. Wilbur had just apologized to me!

I still felt stunned as I followed Mom and

Dad back into the kitchen to unwrap my present. Mom opened the cupboard under the sink and took out the gift I'd been waiting to open. We all sat around the table.

"This is a very special present," said Mom, handing it to me.

"But today you proved you are definitely old enough to use it," said Dad, smiling.

I started to unwrap the long, thin package. What could it be?

"It's a . . . **WAND!**" I screamed, jumping off my chair and into the air. "My very own wand! Thank you!" I said, dancing around the kitchen and waving the wand so that sparks shot out of the star. "It's the best present ever!"

Dad smiled and put his arm around Mom. Mom yawned and leaned her head on Dad. They both closed their eyes.

"We're glad you like it," they murmured sleepily.

Pink Rabbit and I took another slice of cake and wandered back into the great hall on our own. I waved my new wand around, practicing on small things. I changed the colors of the balloons and made one of them do a somersault in the air. Then I sat down next to the pile of presents from my friends.

"It was a fun party overall, wasn't it?" I said, licking the last of the icing off my fingers.

Pink Rabbit nodded.

"I mean, it wasn't perfect," I said. "But I think everything turned out okay in the end. I think my friends enjoyed it. Don't you?"

Pink Rabbit nodded again and snuggled into me.

"It was very kind of Mom and Dad to organize such a nice party for me," I said.

"I am glad they are the way they are. If they were any different, then I wouldn't be me! And I really love being a vampire-fairy."

I pulled the next present onto my lap and started to unwrap it.

"I'm also glad my friends are the way they are," I continued. "They are all very special too."

Pink Rabbit smiled sleepily and yawned.

"I've had a great birthday," I said. "But even so . . . I think I will plan my own party next year!"

PINK
RABBIT

Costume Shop

OPEN

ISADORA LOVES DRESSING UP.
WHAT'S YOUR FAVORITE OUTFIT?

BALLERINA

MERMAID

DINOSAUR

ICE CREAM CONE

PRINCESS

WITCH

ARE YOU MORE FAIRY
OR MORE VAMPIRE?

TAKE THE QUIZ TO FIND OUT!

What's your favorite color?

A. pink   B. black   C. I love them both!

Would you rather go to:

A. a glittery school that teaches magic,
ballet, and making flowery crowns?

B. a spooky school that teaches gliding, bat training,
and how to have the fanciest hair possible?

C. a school where everyone gets to be totally
different and interesting?

On your camping trip, do you:

A. put up your tent with a wave of your
magic wand and go exploring?

B. pop up your fold-out four-poster bed
and avoid the sun?

C. splash around in the sea and have a great time?

RESULTS

Mostly As

You are a glittery, dancing fairy and you love nature!

Mostly Bs

You are a fancy, caped vampire and you love the night!

Mostly Cs

You are half-fairy, half-vampire and totally unique—
just like Isadora Moon!

Family Tree

My Mom,
Countess Cordelia
Moon

Baby Honeyblossom

My Dad,
Count Bartholomew
Moon

Me!
Isadora Moon

Pink Rabbit

Sink your fangs into another Isadora Moon adventure!

ISADORA MOON

Goes to School

Half-fairy, half-vampire, totally unique!

Harriet Muncaster

"Even fairies have to go to school," said Mom.

"Vampires too!" added Dad.

"But I don't *want* to go to school," I said. "I have a perfectly busy and fun life at home with Pink Rabbit."

"But you might enjoy it," insisted Dad. "I used to love my vampire school as a young boy."

"And I adored my fairy school!" said Mom, spooning some flower-nectar yogurt into her bowl.

"You'll have a wonderful time!" They both smiled.

I wasn't so sure.

"But I'm not a full fairy," I said. "And I'm not a full vampire. So which school would I go to? Is there one especially for vampire-fairies? Is there a school for me?"

"Well . . . no," said Mom. "Not exactly."

"You are very rare," said Dad.

"But very special!" added Mom quickly. "And I think fairy school would suit you perfectly."

"But of course you may prefer vampire school," said Dad. "It's a lot more exciting."

Harriet Muncaster

Harriet Muncaster, that's me! I'm the author and illustrator of Isadora Moon.

Yes, really! I love anything teeny-tiny, anything starry, and everything glittery.

New friends. New adventures.
Find a new series ... just for you!

BALLPARK *Mysteries*
THE FENWAY FOUL-UP
FOR THE SPORTS FAN

THE DINO FILES
A Mysterious Egg
FOR THE ADVENTURER

Louise Trapeze
IS TOTALLY 100% FEARLESS
FOR THE SUPERSTAR

PIPER GREEN
PIPER GREEN and the FAIRY TREE
FOR THE DREAMER

PUPPY PIRATES
Stowaway!
FOR THE ANIMAL LOVER

TOTALLY TRUE adventures!
APOLLO 13
FOR THE EXPLORER

RHCBooks.com